A Knock

at the Door

Helen Yeomans

Illustrations by Matteo Mazzacurati

GUARDS PUBLISHING
2015

Published by Guards Publishing, an imprint of Yeomans Associates Ltd.

www.helenyeomans.com

This book is a work of fiction. Names, characters, places and incidents either are the product of the author's imagination or are used fictitiously. Any resemblance to actual persons living or dead, events or locales is entirely coincidental.

Library and Archives Canada Cataloguing in Publication

Yeomans, Helen, 1949-, author

A knock at the door / Helen Yeomans ; illustrations by Matteo Mazzacurati.

Issued in print and electronic formats.

ISBN 978-0-9693219-9-6 (paperback).--ISBN 978-0-9949098-0-0 (ebook)

I. Mazzacurati, Matteo, illustrator II. Title.

PS8647.E65K66 2015   jC813'.6   C2015-906914-9

C2015-906915-7

Cover design www.ivanzanchetta.com

A Knock
at the Door

Contents

The Story of NIGHT

Once upon a time, NIGHT was spelled with just three letters. It was spelled exactly the way it sounded: nuh—eye—tuh.

NIT.

The three letters were good friends. They went everywhere together, especially at NIT. But during the day, they lived in a little house in a lane.

One evening, they had an unexpected visit. It was summer. The sun had set and N, I and T were bustling about getting ready for work—just when most people were relaxing at the end of the day. The birds, who had been up and about since sunrise, were tucking their babies into bed. And the babies, who had spent the entire day learn-

ing to fly by falling out of the nest and then climbing back in and falling out and climbing back. . . . Well, they were so sleepy they could barely keep their eyes open.

In fact, all the birds and all the animals—and most children, too—were snuggling into their beds ready to close their eyes and dream about the adventures they might have tomorrow.

But NIT was a busy time for N, I and T, and they were just putting on their coats when they heard a knock at the door.

N went to open it (she always went first, and I always followed her, and T always followed I), and there on the doormat stood two letters: G and H. They had walked a tremendous long way and they were tired and dusty and footsore. Plus, it was way past their bedtime.

"Please," said H, "is there somewhere we could sleep?"

"It's way past our bedtime," added G.

N, who was kindhearted, was going to welcome them inside when she felt a nudge. I and T were looking at her. It was the sort of look people give other people when they simply have to say something, but don't want to say it in front of the guests.

N turned back to G and H. "Would you excuse us a moment?" she said, and closed the door. She looked at the others. "What's wrong?"

"For one thing," said T, "we're going out in a minute."

"It's way past our bedtime."

4

"And for another," said I, "where would we put them?"

It was a good question. There were only three places G and H could go. They could go in front, in the middle or at the end.

"That's easy," said N. "They can go in front of me! I don't mind."

The others didn't think much of that. N was full of good ideas but they weren't always very practical.

"GHNIT?" said I worriedly. "How can people say GOOD GHNIT?" T said nothing. He just looked at N and shook his head.

"Well, then, they can follow T," said N impatiently.

"NITGH?" I looked even more worried. He was always worrying about something. That's why he was so thin.

"Well, we can't just leave them on the doormat," said N.

T began to pace back and forth, deep in thought. The other two waited, because T was the brains of the group and they all knew it. Suddenly, he stopped.

"What if they were silent?" he said.

I was puzzled. "Silent?"

"Jumping jelly beans," said N. "How could they be si- lent?" She thought it was a preposterous idea; she had never been silent in her entire life.

"Let's see," said T. Quietly he opened the door and they looked outside. Sure enough, there on the doormat were G and H, fast asleep. They just stood there with their eyes closed, propped against each other.

"You see?" said T. "They won't make a sound. And if we put them in the middle, they won't get left behind."

By now, of course, it was nearly dark, so there was no time to argue. They pushed the two letters into place between I and T. When G opened an eye someone said, "Just go back to sleep. Everything's fine." So he did.

In fact, both G and H slept right through till morning, and when they woke up, they were back in the little house in the lane with N, I and T. Well! They were so happy to have found a home that while the others went to bed, they dusted and mopped the whole house and washed the dishes—all before breakfast.

So that's how

NIT

became

NIGHT.

And when you sound it out, don't forget G and H. They're only silent because they're fast asleep.

THE END

The HALF-Trained L

The HAF letters were waiting for an L. A silent L. "We'll have more fun with four of us," said F, and the others agreed.

They had heard the rumours. An L had appeared in HALF in a book in the people world. But they waited and waited and no L came to join them. So they made an appointment to see the head of the L Family.

She listened as they explained the reason for their visit.

Then she gazed at the ceiling. They waited patiently. Eventually, she spoke.

"Ls don't like to be silent," she said.

The three letters did not know what to say to that.

"You have a huge family," said A at last, "and we only want one. Couldn't you just ask around?"

The head of the L Family pondered. Eventually, she agreed to make inquiries.

The three letters walked silently homeward. "What does she mean, she'll 'make inquiries'?" asked F at last. "We have to have an L, don't we?"

The others agreed. "The head of our family would just assign someone," said A.

"Ls are different," said H. "Ls are . . . very full of themselves." He shook his head worriedly.

When they got home, they went to look at the spare

room. It was a depressing sight. There was a dent in one wall and a large fly on the windowsill, with its legs in the air. When they sat on the bed, the metal springs squawked loudly.

H and F decided to paint the room, while A got rid of the fly. After the paint was dry, F stencilled flowers in blue on one wall and H hung a picture over the dent. With a certain amount of grunting and groaning, A, who was quite stout, took the oil can under the bed and oiled the springs.

When they had finished, the spare room no longer looked like a spare room. It looked like the room of someone who actually lived there.

It looked welcoming.

But the days went by and the room stayed empty.

One evening, they heard a knock at the door. They found a small L on the doorstep holding out an envelope. H took it, thanked the messenger and shut the door.

It was a note from the old leader. He read it aloud. "The L Family has been disgraced by L Junior. It would be an excellent punishment for him to spend a hundred years as a silent L. Will you take him? If not, please send him home to his mother."

The three letters puzzled over the last sentence. "How can we send him home?" said F. "We haven't got him."

They remembered the messenger. H threw open the door. There stood the small L, with a belligerent look in his eye.

"L Junior?" asked H.

The small L glared at them and stalked inside. He said nothing when F observed that it had been a fine day. He said nothing when A asked if he'd had his dinner. And he said nothing when they showed him his room. He just walked inside and slammed the door.

"What a stinker!" said F.

"I'll bet he's hungry," said A. So they scrambled some eggs and buttered some toast. Then they marched along to L Junior's room, and marched back again with the small letter between them. They plopped him down at the table.

Now, it had been a difficult day for L Junior, and lunch was a distant memory. When he saw the eggs and the toast (buttered as toast should be buttered, right to the edges)—when he saw all that, and a jar of strawberry jam as well, he couldn't help himself. He ate and ate until the whole lot was inside him, and when he had finished he no longer looked angry. In fact, there was a gleam in his eye when he said "Thank you"—the sort of gleam that means, "Go ahead. Ask me what I did."

So they asked him. And this is what they heard.

Only yesterday, L Junior had been made the leader of LOLLIPOP. This morning, his first day on the job, he left his position at the front and squeezed into the middle of LOLLIPOP, between P and O. And there he stayed, all day long.

H, A and F stared, hardly able to believe their ears.

"It was a joke," explained L Junior.

Lunch was a distant memory.

"You went round all day long as OLLIPLOP?"

"It was just a joke," said L Junior.

The others did not laugh. They got up from the table and backed away from L Junior as though he were a rabid dog. They backed out of the kitchen and kept on backing until they hit the couch. Then they sat down.

H and F wanted to send him home to his mother. "I said he was a stinker," said F.

"Hmm," said A. She stared thoughtfully at the ceiling. Then she stood up and returned to the kitchen and it was ten minutes before she came back.

"He's never been taught. He's never even been in a word before."

The others digested this information. "What did I tell you?" said H finally. "Full of themselves. Imagine sending a letter out without any training!"

16

F began to feel sorry for L Junior. "It's not really his fault. He's too little to know any better."

Eventually, the three letters decided to keep him.

"We're going to train you," said A when they were seated round the kitchen table again. "And then we'll see."

Now, L Junior did not want to be a silent L, not even for a day, never mind a hundred years. But he also didn't want to be treated like a mad dog. He said nothing, but a tear slid down his cheek.

"Maybe you won't have to wait a hundred years," said A, "if you show that you can be reliable."

L Junior looked up at her.

"There are no guarantees," warned H. "You'll have to work hard."

"Could I go back to LOLLIPOP?" More than anything else, he wanted to lead the LOLLIPOP letters again.

"We'll have to see about that," said A, patting his hand.

So L Junior became a silent L in HALF. He set out to learn everything the other letters could teach him. He learned to stay in his place at all times. He learned to be silent. And he learned to watch out for stragglers.

When F was in one of his creative moods, he was the best straggler around. L Junior sometimes spent the entire day pulling on a piece of string, with the other end tied through F's belt to stop him from being left behind.

From A, who was a whiz at arithmetic,

he learned how to count up to twenty-six without using his fingers.

He learned the most from H; not from anything he said, but just from watching him.

H was always there, always ready to help if you were in trouble, or lend a hand if you needed it. L Junior realized after a while that being a good leader meant being reliable and dependable, like H.

The weeks and months went by, then one day the HALF letters were summoned to appear before the head of the L Family. She had heard about L Junior's progress and she was impressed. She was also pleased with H, A and F.

"I have another L for you," she said. F was about to reply that they didn't want another L when A caught his eye with a frown. So he said nothing.

"Has he been causing trouble too?" asked H.

"It's a she," answered the old L. "I don't know what this family is coming to." She looked at L Junior and to his amazement he saw a twinkle in her eye.

He wanted to speak up. He wanted to tell her how much he had learned. But he'd been well-trained, so he said nothing.

However, the other letters did not say nothing.

"We're happy to tell you that L Junior is completely reliable," said H.

"He knows everything we know," added A.

"He'd be a fantastic leader," said F. "He's got imagination."

So it was decided. L Junior said goodbye to his friends and returned to the LOLLIPOP house, where he became a model leader.

As for H, A and F, they were so good at training young Ls

that the head of the family wondered how she had ever managed without them.

Which is why, from that day onward, there has always been a silent L in HALF. It's never the same L from one year to the next, but it's always a stinker.

THE END

The QUIET Strangers

It was a warm summer evening and the KWIET letters were cooking salmon on the barbecue in the backyard. K and W were arguing—the way Ks and Ws always do. K thought the salmon would be cooked in fifteen minutes, but W was sure it would be at least half an hour. They argued back and forth while I looked anxious and E looked hungry and T got more and more annoyed.

Next door, the PEACEFUL letters groaned, because

whenever Ks and Ws disagree (which is most of the time), they do it so loudly that everyone in the neighbourhood can hear.

Finally, T said that if they didn't set the table soon, the salmon would be ready before them. So they hurried back to the house. K led the way, followed by W— still arguing—then I, E and  T. E had to walk twice as fast to keep up because Es have short legs, and since he was a little E, his legs were even shorter.

They collected the corn on the cob and the baked potatoes and the salt and butter, and the plates and knives and forks, and returned outside to the barbecue.

The picnic table had room for five letters on each side, so they set five places along one side of the table and put a corn on the cob and a potato on each plate. By this time the salmon was ready.

"Excuse us?"

Two letters were standing near the side of the house. "We knocked at the door," said one, and the other added, "but nobody heard." Then they both spoke together: "How far is it to the nearest inn?"

"Three miles," said W, but K was positive it was four, and they began to argue while the two strangers watched curiously.

E looked longingly at the salmon. When you're hungry and dinner is on the table, the last thing you want is interruptions.

"Won't you join us for dinner?" invited T.

Two letters stood near the side of the house.

The strangers hesitated.

"We have lots," said K.

"No—" W began to disagree, then just in time she remembered her manners. "Yes, we do."

The strangers came to the table. They were a Q and a U, dusty from their travels.

"Would you like to wash up?" asked W.

"No thank you," they said together, looking hungrily at the food, so the seven letters sat down to dinner. The two strangers sat opposite the KWIET letters, sharing a plate between them.

For a while there was silence, except for the sort of sounds letters make when they're really enjoying their food. I was the first to finish.

"Have you come a long way?" she asked.

"Many hundreds of miles," said Q, because U had his

mouth full. He went on to say that they came from a land of sun and sand and camels.

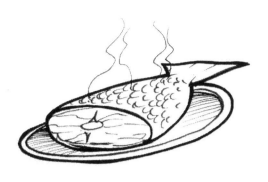

E had never seen a Q before. "Aren't you in a word?" he asked as he scraped up the last bit of potato and melted butter on his plate.

"We would like to be," said Q, and U added, "but only if we can stay together."

"What sound do you make?" asked T.

"Qw," said Q and U.

The KWIET letters stared at them.

"But—but—but—" stuttered K.

"That's our sound!" W was puzzled. "How did you do that? How can a U make a W sound?"

"We do it together," said Q and U. And they did it again: "Qw."

"That doesn't really sound like us," said K, but W knew it sounded exactly the same and they got into another argument.

I gazed at the strangers. They seemed to be very good friends. They always agreed with each other. And they spoke so softly! I decided she liked them.

She nudged E with her elbow and they climbed down from the picnic table. (This isn't easy to do when you're in the middle, so I went first because she was thinner.) They walked round and sat down next to Q and U. Then E wriggled with excitement because T came round and joined them!

Q and U looked very worried at this, but T smiled. "Let's give it a try," he said.

There was some clearing of throats and a cough or two, and then:

"Quiet," said the five letters, all together.

Across the table, K and W stopped arguing. They looked round and found themselves alone. They were so startled that they fell over backwards, right off the bench.

"You can't do that!" said K as they picked themselves up. Now Q and U looked really worried. "We should leave," they said together and began to rise.

But T told them to sit down, and turned to K and W. "You said you'd like to do more SKIING," he said to K. The SKIING letters were looking for a permanent replacement for their K, who had broken his leg and decided KNITTING suited him better. "So now you can go SKIING all day long."

K pondered.

"What about me?" said W.

"You always wanted to join your sister in WINDOW, remember?"

K and W looked at each other. "He's right," said K.

W wasn't quite convinced.

"Are you sure you don't mind?" she asked the two strangers.

Mind? Q and U looked at each other. They had been invited to dinner by these hospitable letters. Now they were being invited to stay forever. E gazed at them brightly, his short legs swinging back and forth. I and T were smiling at them.

"We would love to stay," said Q and U together.

"Perfect!" said K. He turned to W. "Shall we take the plates in first? Then we can come back for the rest."

"An excellent suggestion, my dear K," said W, and they picked up the plates and went off to the house without arguing once.

The QUIET letters sat at the table smiling at each other the way letters do when they know they're going to get along. They decided to practice one more time.

"Quiet," they said, all together. A scuffling noise made them turn around. The PEACEFUL letters were looking over the fence. They peered at Q and U in the evening light, nudging and grinning and whispering among themselves. Finally, one of them spoke.

"Welcome to the neighbourhood," said the leader of PEACEFUL.

So QUIET has always begun with QU, ever since that day long ago when two strangers from a distant land found a home where they could always be together.

THE END

PIGEON Panic

Os can be silly letters, giggling and fooling around, especially when they're together. However, just because most Os are knuckleheads doesn't mean they all are.

The O in PIGEON, for example, was quite a sensible letter—maybe because he had no other Os to play with. When the PIGEON letters got into trouble one day, it was O who knew what the problem was. Unfortunately, no one would listen to him.

It really began when the old G in PIGEON died and a new one took his place. Letters live a very long time—about ten times as long as people—but eventually the old G died and went to OED. (This is pronounced "weed" and it's where all letters go when they die.)

One day, not long after joining PIGEON, the new G became confused and forgot what sound to make. "Pigeon" started coming out as "piggon" instead, and the PIGEON letters began to panic.

That evening, as they climbed up to their tree-house in the old oak tree, O tried to get E's attention. He knew she should be helping G to make the right sound. But E spent all her time daydreaming. He gave her a nudge. "I'd rather have raspberry jelly," she said in a dreamy sort of way.

O turned to N behind him. "I know what's wrong," he began, but N ignored him.

Just then, the EAGLE letters went by, climbing up to their house at the top of the tree. "Piggon?" they said scornfully. "Good grief!"

G hung his head and P was mortified.

They hastened inside and shut the door. Without even stopping for supper, they began to practice. But G became more and more confused, and finally they flopped down on the sofa to rest. O did backflips and made faces at E. But E just gazed at the ceiling through her long, long eyelashes, lost in a daydream.

Suddenly there came a thunderous bang at the door, and the whole tree-house shook. Before they could move an inch, the door burst open and in came a— Well, no one knew quite what it was, or how it came in. Did it whirl or roll or twirl or flip? Or did it do all these things and more besides? It looked like a tornado—a green tornado—and it stopped in front of the PIGEON letters.

"Gee whiz!" said O, bouncing up and down.

"G Wiz is acceptable," the tornado agreed. "I am the G Wizard." It stopped whirling about and became a short fat G in a long green cape and a huge, lopsided hat. Two hands reached up and grasped the rim of the hat. They tugged and the hat straightened. A face looked back at them.

"You're not ENOUGH," said the G Wizard. She began to rummage in a pocket.

"We're PIGEON," said the letters.

"I can see that." She pulled out a scrap of paper. It was a list of appointments. "Oh. Yes. An emergency." She looked at the PIGEON letters. "What seems to be the problem?"

G blushed, and the G Wizard seemed to know instantly. "Ah. Piggon?"

P nodded glumly and everyone began talking at once.

"I used to be leader of GET," explained G, "and I don't know why I started saying 'guh' instead of 'juh', but now I'm so confused."

I suddenly jumped to his feet and said it was too much to

expect him to remind G when he had his own sound to think about. He flung himself back on the couch and burst into tears.

"All right, all right. Keep your shirt on," said the G Wizard.

"It's my fault," said P, patting I's shoulder. "I keep turning round to help G and it just seems to make things worse."

"You can't do everything," said the G Wizard. She thought deeply for a moment. "What about adding a D, like WIDGEON or FUDGE?" she asked. "Then D and G could help each other."

The PIGEON letters didn't care for that idea. "We like being different," said P, and the others nodded.

"Well? Why call me? Are you expecting a Magic Solution?"

"We didn't call you—" began P.

"I don't do Magic Solutions," she went on. "I just help letters to express themselves." She began to pace back and forth, one finger tapping her chin. She stopped in front of G.

"If you don't want to learn a new sound, why did you leave GET?"

G looked at E, and then gazed bashfully at the floor. The G Wizard suddenly noticed O, who was making horrible faces and pointing at E.

And what was E doing? She was still daydreaming, gazing into space.

"Oh brother," said the G Wizard. "You! E!"

E came back to earth. "Yes?" she said vaguely.

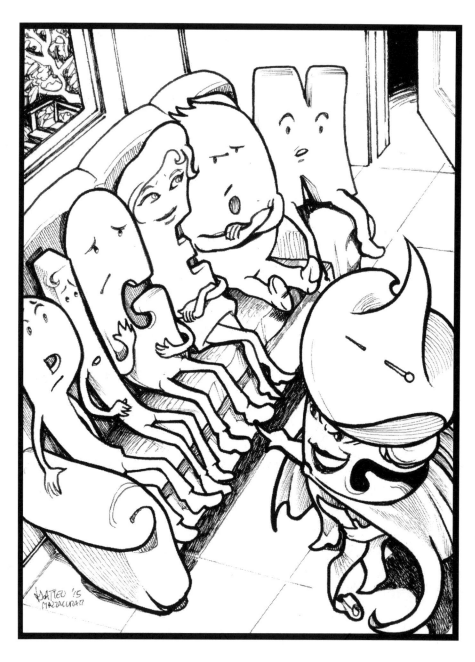

"I just help letters to express themselves."

"You and G should work together. Can't you just give him a nudge and remind him he's a 'juh' sound?"

E looked helpless. "Oh, I couldn't do that," she said. "I'm too busy."

"Busy? Busy? Doing what?"

"I have a lot to think about."

O rolled his eyes. "She wants to be in TELEVISION."

"TELEVISION?" The G Wizard frowned. "Why?"

"Because she's so beautiful," said G. O looked for somewhere to throw up.

"Well?" The G Wizard looked at E. "What's stopping you?"

"They haven't any openings right now."

"Hmm. TELEVISION." She began to pace again, then stopped suddenly. "And when they do," she asked, "what makes you think they'll want you?"

This had never occurred to E. How could anyone not want her?

"Being a word takes teamwork," said the G Wizard. "Why would the TELEVISION letters take someone who just sits there like a lump on a log?"

O hooted with laughter and rolled into E, who pushed him away.

"You should be helping G, not daydreaming," said the G Wizard. She stopped pacing and began to fiddle with her hat, muttering to herself. "Where is it? Aha!" She withdrew a long hatpin and held it up. The point twinkled.

"This is a hatpin," she said, unnecessarily. She held it out to E. "I always carry a spare. Keep it with you at all times, and whenever you feel yourself drifting off, just give yourself a little poke."

E looked as though she might faint. "I couldn't do that," she said. "I might hurt myself."

"Give it to me," said O helpfully. "I'll do it."

The G Wizard looked at E. "Would you like him to help?"

"Are you serious?" E sat up straight and took the hatpin.

"Right!" said the G Wizard, "no more 'piggon'." She stepped back and looked at each letter in turn. Then she nodded briskly to P. "Remember," she said, "teamwork. That's the key." And with that, she turned into a tornado again and whirled away. The door banged shut behind her.

P sat there with his mouth open. "Teamwork?" he said at last.

"Exactly," said I and N nodded, while O did a somersault.

G looked at E and E looked at the hatpin. "If you could just remind me . . ." began G and E looked up. "You can count on it," she said. They looked at the others, then said together, "Teamwork."

The PIGEON letters never had a problem after that, because G and E worked together to make a "juh" sound. In fact, they became such a good team that E has completely forgotten about TELEVISION.

Every now and then, O asks her to show him the hatpin. "Over my dead body," she always says. In his spare time, O practices whizzing round like a tornado. He wants to be a wizard when he grows up, and have hatpins of his own.

THE END

The Beginning of BOUGH

There are lots of twins in the Letter World, and they usually stay together when they join a word. The Gs in WAGGLE are twins. So are the Ps in MUPPET, and the Ls in BRILLIANT.

But sometimes in an emergency, twins have to be split up. This happened one day in the year 1500, when the first two letters in BODY fell sick and had to be replaced. The only letters available were twins, so one B and one O left their homes to join BODY.

A few days later, the stay-at-home B paid a visit to the BODY household. He found the other O there as well, playing with her brother.

"Guess what?" said the BODY letters. "The house next door is empty. If you find a word, you could move in."

B and O discussed this on the way home. What word could they be?

"BOO," said O. Another O to play with; she liked that idea.

"Already a word," said B.

"Well . . . BOOT . . . BOTTOM . . . BONNET . . . BOTTLEWASHER."

At each word, B shook his head, till finally, O said, "Well, you think of a word."

B thought for a while. "Boozlewoofer," he said at last.

"Oooooh!" O was hugely impressed. "With four Os?" she asked, and B realized this could be a problem. Four Os in one word might be more than he could manage.

Along the road towards them came a word: ROUGH.

"We're starting a new word," announced O. "Boozlewoofer."

"Congratulations," said the ROUGH letters. "What does it mean?"

"I don't know," admitted B. "I just made it up."

The two Os began to play push and shove. R said, "Wouldn't it be more fun to be in a word that people actually use?"

B gazed at the ROUGH letters. "Rough," he said in a thinking-out-loud voice.

"That's us," said R.

"Buff," said B. "B-O-U-G-H."

U clapped his hands and G and H nodded. "Very clever."

R wasn't so sure. "Do you think people would change," he asked doubtfully, "if they're used to B-U-F-F?"

"Boozlewoofer!" yelled O. "I like boozlewoofer."

"Boozlewoofer would need two sets of twins," said R. "There wouldn't be room for you."

O stared at him. If she stuck out her tongue and her

dad found out, she'd be in deep trouble. Instead, she did six backflips in a straight line down the road to show what she thought of R. She ended up under a great oak tree and H suddenly said, "BOGH." He pronounced it "bow" as in bow-wow.

"What's that?"

"The branch of a tree," explained H. "B-O-G-H. My great-grandfather's in BOGH. They're all really, really old and they want to retire. You could take over."

"It would look better with a U in it," said U.

"Bough?" B thought about it. U was right. "BOUGH!" he said firmly, and suddenly hopped up and down. "Yes! B-O-U-G-H," he explained as O came back walking on her hands. "A tree branch."

"Whatever." O wasn't saying anything else in front of R.

The ROUGH letters wished them good luck and continued on their way. "The Council of Letters can help," called back H, just as they disappeared around a bend in the road.

The Council of Letters consists of the heads of all the twenty-six letter families. It meets once a month, and B realized today was the meeting day.

"That's a good idea," he said. "We can ask them about a U and a G and an H."

"My dad says the Council of Letters is a bunch of old fogies," said O. Seeing the look on B's face, she added, "But I won't say that to them."

When they got to town, they found the Council of Letters playing bowls (a game like bowling, but played on grass) on the Common. The head of the V Family, oldest of all the leaders, sat dozing in the sun.

The U leader was waiting to take his turn. B and O explained what they wanted.

"U-G-H?" he asked. "Hmm. I know where you can get an O-U-G-H. Ouch!" he added as O did a backflip and accidentally landed on his foot.

"Sorry," said O insincerely.

"We just want a U and a G and an H," said B. The U leader took his turn and bowled the ball and the other family heads applauded. The ancient V leader woke up. "Fine work," he said. "Very, very fine" and dozed off again.

The U leader went to consult with some of the other family heads. He returned with the leaders of G, H and O.

"We have an O-U-G-H for you," said the head of the O Family, "and I have a new word for you . . ." she smiled at O, "with two other Os. It's—"

"No!" said B and O together.

O looked at B in surprise. "Do you mean that?"

"Course I do," answered B. He turned to the four leaders. "We started this word together. We're staying together."

O was so pleased her face turned pink and she scowled at the O leader and said the first thing that came into her head. "Boozlewoofer."

The four leaders exchanged a look. The head of the G family spoke first. "I think they'll be fine," he said. The other three agreed, and promised B and O the new letters

"We just want a U and a G and an H."

would meet them tomorrow morning at the fork in the road.

"Are you in the Book?" asked the head of the H Family. She meant the Book of Words, which is like a telephone book without the phone numbers. It lists all known words and their addresses. It is kept up-to-date by the Recorder.

B had forgotten about the Book of Words.

"Better register right away," advised the G leader, "before someone else does."

The Recorder lived in a tall, thin house in a street of tall, thin houses. B and O knocked at the door, then waited and waited. They knocked again. At last the door opened and an old, bent R peered at them from under bushy eyebrows.

"Well? What is it?" he asked impatiently.

"We're starting a new word. Bough."

"Meaning?"

"A tree branch."

"Already taken." He be-
gan to close the door.

"But it's a new way of
spelling it. B-O-U-G-H,"
spelled B desperately, and
just as the door was about
to latch shut, it stopped moving.

The two letters waited, hardly daring to breathe. At last,
the door opened a crack more. "B-O-U-G-H. Branch of a
tree." The Recorder scrutinized them from under his shaggy
eyebrows. "Why did you choose that spelling?"

O did a backflip. "We like having a U," she said when she
was right way up.

"Where are the rest of you?"

"They're coming tomorrow," answered B.

At last the door opened wide. "Come in," said the Recorder, and they followed him into the house and up a flight of stairs, round a corner and up another flight. At the top, he entered an attic room with a sloped ceiling.

The room was filled with books, shelves and shelves and stacks and stacks of them. B had never seen so many books. He liked the smell of them.

On a table next to a window sat the Book of Words. It was really not so much a book as a thick stack of pages held together with three leather loops or bands on one side.

The Recorder sat down at the table and pulled the Book towards him. He opened it and began leafing through the pages. "Branch of a tree," B heard him mutter. "Ah. Here we are: BOGH."

B peered over his shoulder. There it was: BOGH. Followed by an address: 2 Whyte Cliffe Down.

"That is a very old word," said the Recorder. "And people are getting tired of it."

"How do you know?" B asked.

The Recorder held up a finger: Wait. Slowly he rose to his feet and with hands clasped behind his back, proceeded to walk slowly past the shelves of books, peering occasionally at a title. He came to the corner where the sloped roof was highest. Here a stepladder leaned against the shelves. He climbed the ladder and reached out to pluck a book from the middle of the second-highest shelf. He brought it back to the table and opened it. "Look."

B and O bent over the book. The Recorder's finger pointed at a word on page 30. The two letters looked at each other in amazement. The word was "bough."

"Address?"

"But we just made it up!"

"I expect the writer decided 'bough' looks better with a U. If you hadn't knocked at my door, I would have had to ask the Council of Letters for volunteers for a new word."

They watched as he added BOUGH to the right place in the Book of Words. "Address?"

"It's next to BODY," said B. "On the Old Forest Road."

The Recorder turned the pages until he found BODY— 6700 Old Forest Road. "Are you to the right or left, facing their house?"

"We're to the right," said B and O, and the Recorder entered: 6701 Old Forest Road. Then he put down his quill pen and gazed at them. "Congratulations." And he bowed very formally to them both.

Bright and early the following morning, B arrived at the fork in the road. He was wearing his two sets of clothes and carried a sack with all his belongings in it. O

arrived soon after. "I've got five sandwiches and five ap-

ples," she announced.

Along the road from town came the other three letters. H

had on two sets of clothes as well, and he carried his favourite

possession, a pewter whistle shaped like a chicken. G was pull-

ing a small wagon loaded with

belongings and food, and U

had a bowl with two guppies in

it.

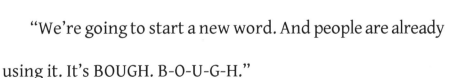

The five letters met and

introduced themselves. It was

an exciting moment, and B

felt he ought to make a speech.

"We're going to start a new word. And people are already

using it. It's BOUGH. B-O-U-G-H."

U put down the bowl of guppies and clapped while O did two backflips and G and H shouted "Hooray!"

"I think we should take a moment to practice," B went on, and the others hastily got into line and paid attention.

"Let's remember: We're not 'uff' like rough, or 'off' like cough. We're not 'oo' like through, or 'aw' like thought. We're not even 'oh' like though." He looked at the others. "What are we?"

"We're 'ow'," said O, U, G and H.

Then all together, they said, "We're BOUGH."

"And we're going to be BOUGH for . . ." B's imagination took flight ". . . for a thousand years!"

He may be right. The BOUGH letters have been together now for 515 years, and they still live in the house at 6701 Old Forest Road, next to BODY.

THE END

Did You Like It?

If you enjoyed *A Knock at the Door*, how about saying so? Maybe on the website where your copy came from. Some people call this "writing a review," but don't let that stop you. Just pick one of the sentences on the next page and finish it off.

My Book Review

I really liked this book because _____

_____

I LOVED this book because _____

_____

This book is silly because letters can't talk. But I STILL

liked it because _____

_____

Other Words?

If you can think of other words who might like their stories told, the author would like to know. You can reach her at: knock@helenyeomans.com

Manufactured by Amazon.ca
Bolton, ON

18855279R00042